For my children,

Reginald, Dominique, Tiffany, Noble, Andreu,
Quesette, Jordan, Jonathan, Mia Faye and the village,
you must know where you came from
in order to know where you are going.

Loving you always,

Ya Ya

DOMINIQUE AND THE MIRROR
Book 2: THE CARPENTER

© Cassie, 2017
All rights reserved.

ISBN-13: 978-0-692-05016-3
ISBN-10: 0692050167

Printed in the United States of America

Dominique
and the Mirror

Book 2

THE CARPENTER

---

by

Cassie

Illustrations by

Amakubukuro Brown

Hi, it's Dominique again.

On Tuesday morning a year after my trip to High Point, North Carolina, where I met Sarah at the family gathering, "It happened again!" I did not see myself in the mirror as I was getting ready for school. I saw a man! The man looked like a carpenter. I carefully watched him as he carved a large oval. I knew that this man was a slave because of the scars around his wrists and his neck, which were caused by iron shackles. After he finished the carving on the round piece of wood, he put a wooden container with a long wooden stick on the table close to the oval he was carving. There was gold colored paint and the stick was a hand-made paint brush. He then started to paint the oval carving, he waited for a while and then he touched the frame, testing it to make sure it was dry.

The mirror showed me how the man looked around to see if anyone was watching him, he pulled out a small piece of paper and what looked like a black pencil. As this man was writing in his native language, he spoke the words that sounded like a prayer. "God this is Adedayo, thank you for the power and many blessings you put upon me to make this mirror. I dedicate this mirror to you Lord and your goodness that my offering of this mirror will save and protect my family, with all praises and glory to the God of Abraham, Amen." He then folded the very small paper and inserted it into the painted frame where no one could see it, and then he inserted the glass mirror.

I realized at that moment it looked like my mirror! And as suddenly as my mirror showed me the Carpenter, it then showed my reflection. I was stunned but so excited! It's happening again! I had so many questions, who was this slave, am I seeing 1862 again? I came to the conclusion that the carpenter must be an ancestor just as Sarah was.

When I came home from school, I saw in the mirror more information about the carpenter. His name was Adedayo. The mirror showed me he was given the name of Joseph when he was auctioned to the Shepard's when he was led off the ship from Africa to the auction house. "The Shepard's"! That was the name of the people's house my dad renovated that gave him the mirror.

I kept watching the mirror and noticed Adedayo used the name Joseph when he was in the presence of the slave master or overseer. The mirror showed me how Adedayo refused to give up his identity, his inner strength or his culture. He carefully watched what was going on around him. He saw that if slaves showed their inner strengths in their situation, they were either badly beaten with a whip or killed.

Adedayo taught himself how to hide his strengths. He realized he alone could not help himself or others because he was always outnumbered. By doing this, his capturers would think he was as docile as the other captives who had accepted their situation of being slaves, but he had not and never would accept being a slave.

The mirror continued to show me how Adedayo who was now called Joseph, taught himself to read and write the English language. He taught himself from the pages of a newspaper given to him by the master. It had a picture of a mirror for sale that the master told him to make. Adedayo knew it was an automatic death sentence for any slave caught reading or writing. He paid attention to everything around him without being noticed. At night he remembered his homeland, his father the king, his mother the queen and the elders of his tribe. The mirror showed my reflection again. I questioned why the mirror was showing me how Sarah's father was captured. I went to bed with this question on my mind.

The next day, I prepared for school and saw in the mirror that Adedayo was a 20-year-old man who was captured in the land of his kingdom which is now called Nigeria on the Continent of Africa. The mirror showed me the elders of his tribe. The mirror then showed me where the elders saw three black birds flying over the village three times in a circle. They were gifted with the seeing. They told the royal family there was a problem coming to the village. They said it was because their ancestors disobeyed God's law when they worshiped a golden idol as their God. I wondered if the elders were referring to the Egyptians letting the Hebrew slaves free in the Bible. The elders warned Adedayo that death was coming to him. They continued to say that he would experience the death of his present life and then he would be born anew through a great past ancestor in three new lands. Adedayo did not understand this. He was then told to stay close to the village, be didn't listen. The mirror showed my reflection again. I went to school.

When I came home from school, the mirror just showed my reflection. It was not until late that night the mirror showed how Adedayo was overlooking the land of his father's village with one of his childhood friends when he went into the seeing. God spoke to Adedayo telling him while he was in the seeing, "You will bring me and my word into three foreign lands". No one knew when he was in the seeing. He looked and acted normal. Suddenly, I saw men coming from everywhere, I yelled, "Adedayo watch out!" Adedayo and his friend were surrounded by nine men who were of a complexion they had never seen before. He and his childhood friend fought gallantly. The men overpowered Adedayo and his friend, put them in chains and took them away. The mirror shut down. "Wow"! "They were kidnapped!" My mom told me to go to sleep, and I did.

The next morning

the mirror did not show anything but my reflection. I thought about what happened all day and rushed home after school. When I looked in the mirror I saw his capturers take Adedayo and his friend to a place where he was chained around the neck, wrists, and ankles. I watched as they put him in a room that was dark, that looked like a jail cell I had once seen on the T.V. It appeared that Adedayo and the others were in this place for many months. The mirror showed my reflection again. I started to look in books I borrowed from the library and found a picture of the place they took Adedayo and his friend to. It's called Goree Island. My book says it is outside of Dakar in Africa. I read more. This is a real place! The book said Goree Island today is called The Maison des Esclaves (The door of no return). It was one of the shipping ports used to hold captives for the journey to America.

There, each captured person was branded with a hot iron (like they do to animals, proving who own them). I continued to read and the book said, if these people survived after months of imprisonment in that place, they would then be walked through the "door of no return" onto ships to America's and other countries where they were sold at auction. "I was actually watching the African holocaust. This really happened to people!" The mirror showed my reflection again.

I ran home after school again to look in the mirror. Without fail, the mirror continued to show me the terrible way Adedayo and the other captured people were treated. This was a terrible way to learn a lesson for not listening, and for not doing what you were told. The mirror then showed two men taking Adedayo and others from the dark room through a brick hallway in his prison to a large black door. The man opened the door to the blinding sunlight, and after Adedayo's eyes adjusted he saw a huge boat in the ocean which many people were being led onto.

The mirror showed me it was a voyage that took many months. The countless numbers of captured people were housed in the bowel of the ship packed together, it was unbearable. The mirror showed me that Adedayo survived, most of his fellow countrymen, women, and children were not so lucky.

The ship after months at sea arrived in America. Adedayo and others were led off the ship to a land that had stone everywhere they walked. He saw buildings he had never seen before. All the people he saw were of the same skin color, and their bodies were covered with many layers of clothes as the men who had captured him. The mirror showed my reflection again and I went to school.

After school, I came home and saw that men were leading Adedayo and others to a building that was square and not round as in his village. Adedayo was walked up steps where these people who captured him, called him Joseph and allowed other men to touch and examine him as though he was a horse or a cow. They were yelling words Adedayo did not understand. "One hundred, two hundred, three hundred, sold!" Sold to the Shepard plantation! And then he was taken away by others of the same complexion to another place by something attached to some kind of large animal he had never seen before. Once they arrived at this strange place, Adedayo and others were handed over to another man. This man fed and taught them the ways of a plantation.

The overseer took him to a place that was made of wood, dark inside and had a floor of earth. He told him this will be your home and your women. This is where he met his wife, Sadie. He did not understand what the overseer was saying because of the language difference. With the help of Sadie his wife, she taught him the way he was to live in this new land.

Dominique remembered what the elders of his village said to him "There was death coming to him, the death of his present life. And then he would be born anew through a great past ancestor in three new lands". She recognized what she was seeing. It was the first land Adedayo was told he would travel too. Suddenly, Dominique understood that this was Sarah's father. Dominique said out loud, "Adedayo is a member of my family! He created the mirror that shows me my family and our history of where we come from!"

The End

For Now...

www.ingramcontent.com/pod-product-compliance
Lightning Source LLC
Chambersburg PA
CBHW041008170626
46815CB00002B/207

9780692050163